Ms. Blanche, the Spotless Cow

by Zidrou ◆ illustrated by David Merveille

Henry Holt and Company ◆ New York

All the cows in Farmer Goodfellow's meadow had spots. All except Ms. Blanche. Poor thing! She wanted so much to have spots like the other cows.

"A cow without spots," she mooed mournfully, "is like Santa Claus without a beard."

But a beard will grow.
A spot will not.

"Quit chewing over your troubles like this, Blanche,"
said Mr. Goodfellow, the farmer. "At least there are
no spots in your milk."
   Ms. Blanche didn't laugh.

One day a traveling salesman came to the town where Ms. Blanche lived.

"Come one, come all," he cried. "I sell the stuff that dreams are made of."

Ms. Blanche seized her chance. "I beg your pardon, sir," she said politely. "Do you also sell spots?"

"Spots?" cried the salesman. "I sell nothing *but* spots.
I am the greatest spot-seller in the world."

The salesman had a very large selection of spots.

But none of them really pleased Ms. Blanche.

The days went by, as days do. Ms. Blanche grew sadder and sadder.

Then, on a beautiful spring morning, an artist planted his easel in Ms. Blanche's meadow. The artist set to work happily. But his inspiration soon disappeared when he heard Ms. Blanche's constant mooing.

He decided to take matters into his own hands.
Ms. Blanche was spotless no more.

(To our knowledge, this is the first documented instance of cow painting in the history of art.)

He painted a great spot.
A little too great even.
Because the painter was famous.
Very famous indeed.

Soon people came from all over
to admire Ms. Blanche's spot.

The director of the Extremely Modern Art Museum of Gotta-Havit, U.S.A., offered five million dollars to Farmer Goodfellow for the piece. "But I want the hide, not the cow," said the director. "We've already done a cow show in our gallery."

Farmer Goodfellow was tempted.
What would he do?

Before he could answer, a large rain cloud
passed overhead, deciding Ms. Blanche's fate.
Her spot was, as you've guessed, watercolor.
(Artists can be very famous without being
very clever.)

Ms. Blanche gave up hope. There would never be a spot for her. Just tears, a real stream of tears.

When the storm cleared, Farmer Goodfellow had an idea. "I think it is high time you became acquainted with my liveliest bull," he said.

The bull was nice looking. A little rough.
But so very nice looking.
And what should happen happened.

In a meadow, a cow.
Beside the cow, a calf.
A happy calf.
In a meadow, a cow.
A smiling cow.
A happy cow.
You know why!

Happiness, often, depends on so little.
On a little Spot, for instance.

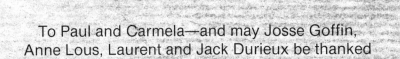

To Paul and Carmela—and may Josse Goffin,
Anne Lous, Laurent and Jack Durieux be thanked

First American edition
ISBN 0-8050-2550-2

Printed in E.E.C.

1 3 5 7 9 10 8 6 4 2